YOU CAN LOOK ALL THAT
YOU WANT BUT
SOME OF THEM
WILL NEVER
BE
FOUND!

ONWARD SOCKS!

IAN
KLEPETAR

Dedicated to Finlay, Liam, and all the missing socks of the world. May you be wild and free and if you happen to find your match, stay true to you.

Printed in the United States of America

First Printing, 2018

ISBN 978-0-9998865-0-2

Limitless Publishing
www.limitlessbooks.us

Where Do Missing Socks Go?

...Wouldn't you like to know?

Words by Ian Klepetar
Pictures by Danielle Marino

Limitless
Books
Publishing

They were worn as a pair just hours ago.
Now I have one, where'd the other one go?

So I said to myself, it's for sure on the floor,
where I'd taken them off just moments before.

No sock
around,
no clues
in sight,
they must
disappear,
what they say
must be right!

"But, wait a minute!"
I said while I squirmed under my bed,
an interesting thought
popped into my head...

What if the socks that we lose
every day were not lost at all
but were running away?!

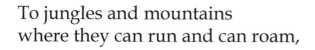

To jungles and mountains
where they can run and can roam,

In a place where short sox
and long sox can call home.

Where the air is made
up of smells and
strong stenches,

And the places to rest
are upon lost shoe benches.

11

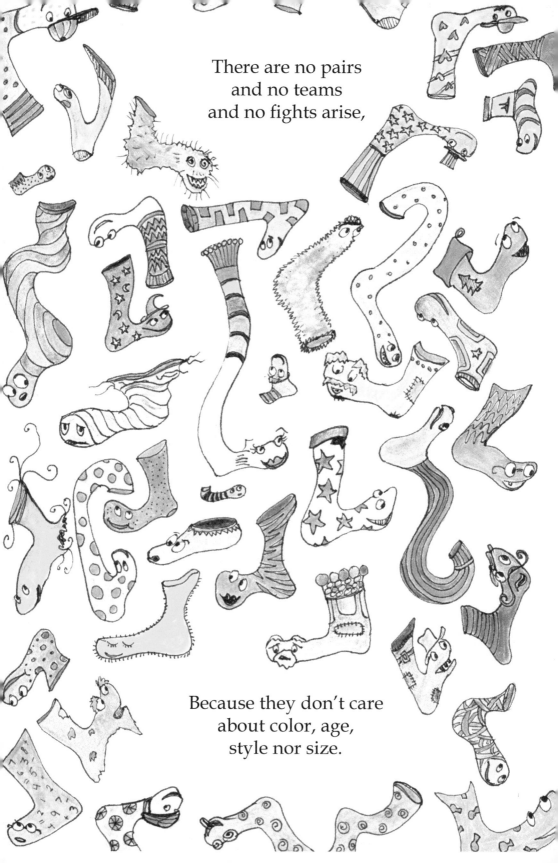

There are no pairs
and no teams
and no fights arise,

Because they don't care
about color, age,
style nor size.

There's socks with big holes,

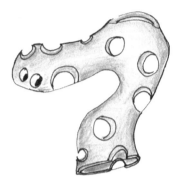

And threads ready to pull,

There are new socks,

And old socks,

Silk, Cotton, and Wool!

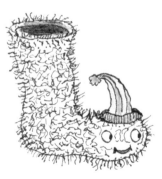

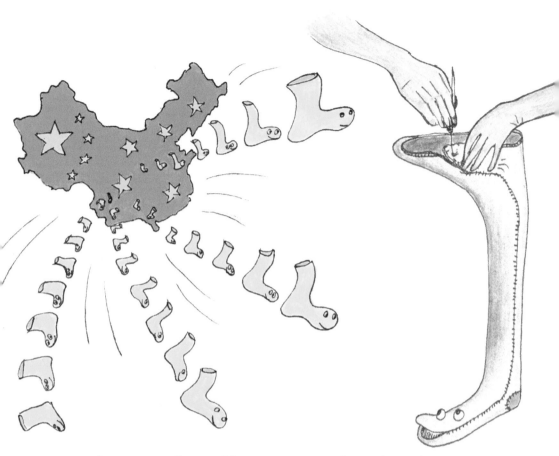

Some made in China, some others hand sewn,
Some have elastic and with others it's blown.

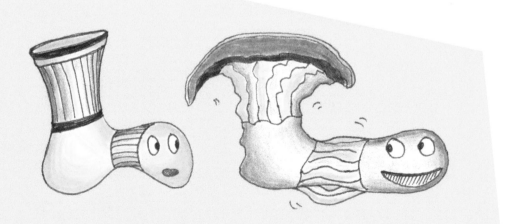

There's
hole
in the
heel
socks,

There's
hole
in the
toe
socks.

There's thick socks, there's thin socks,
There's covered in mold socks.

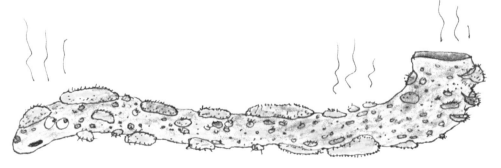

There are striped socks and white socks,

Polka-dot spots galore!

There's zig zags and zag zigs,

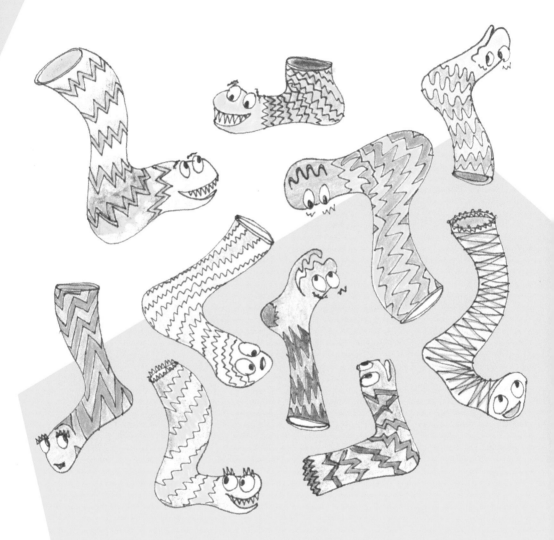

It's mismatched and more!

There are brown socks and blue socks,
Pink and purple for sure,

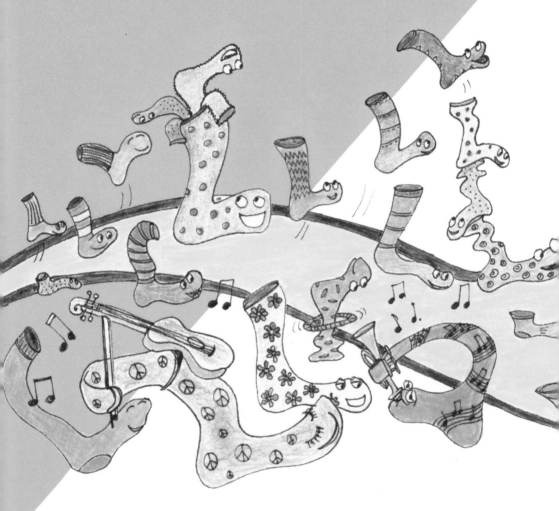

There's orange socks and red sox,
Tye-dyed socks on tour.

Free of cars, planes or buses to tote them around,
The heel and toe combo is the best they have found.

No need for gadgets or gizmos to keep
these socks entertained, they dance and
they party and cannot be contained!

21

They run and they play and live out their days,
With no feet attached they can go their own ways.

When they're worn out from all their sock fun,
They rinse off in the rain and dry off in the sun.

23

Soon tuckered out
and ready to sleep,
They all pile up in an
unmatched sock heap.

When they are
sleeping some
will be taken,
picked up and
removed from
their sock filled
vacation.

They go to a place that single socks know,
Those seeking matches when they are ready to go.

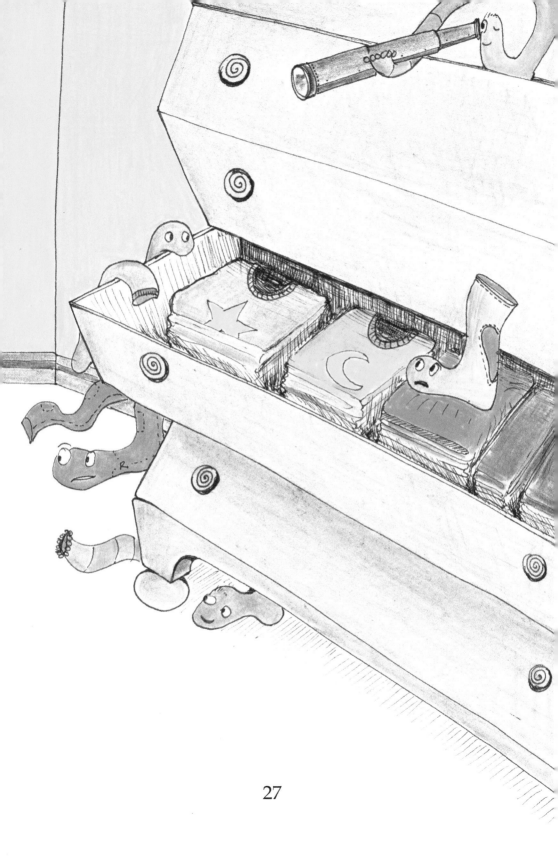

Though there's no need to worry,
A new adventure's begun,
In this paired up sock world,
Two's can be just as fun!

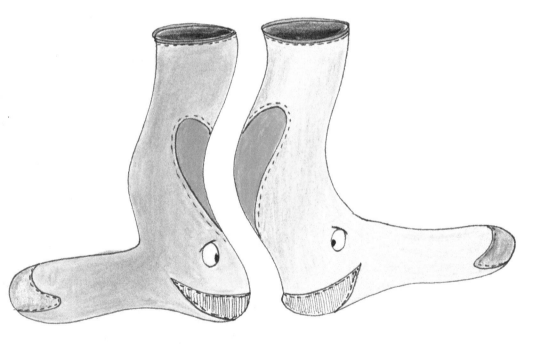

The Beginning...

Ian is happiest when playing in the mountains, jumping into water and off on running or biking adventures. His greatest passion is bringing ideas, tools and projects into the world which inspire fun, personal connections, and positive growth. He lives a nomadic lifestyle, loves his family, friends and his work as the founding director of Bicycle Benefits, a national organization.

Danielle is a joyous adventurer, nature lover and artist. She always has a crayon in her pocket! Her dreams of being an "inventor" are now being realized as she explores a career in sustainable and regenerative design. She hopes that readers will be inspired to follow their true paths and live a life that is well-balanced, conscious, and full of adventure.

Draw your favorite sock!

Write a sock tale!

31

CPSIA information can be obtained
at www.ICGtesting.com
Printed in the USA
BVHW02*2106080618
518024BV00003B/1/P

9 780999 886502